STAR PAWS

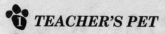

PUPPY PATROL
STAR PAWS

JENNY DALE

Illustrations by Mick Reid
Cover illustration by Michael Rowe

AN
APPLE
PAPERBACK

SCHOLASTIC INC.
New York Toronto London Auckland Sydney
Mexico City New Delhi Hong Kong

SPECIAL THANKS TO HELEN MCGEE

ISBN 0-439-11327-X

12 11

4 5/0

Printed in the U.S.A.

40

First Scholastic printing, April 2000

CHAPTER ONE

Prince raced across the beach, ears back, fur flying in the wind.

"Wait for me!" Zeno yelled. "You can't go without me, Prince!"

The golden cocker spaniel turned his head and barked.

"I am *hurrying*," Zeno said breathlessly, pounding after the dog.

Behind them, thundering through the shallows, the runners of their sand skimmers spraying seawater, came the Xarcons.

Zeno stumbled on a rock and fell, sprawling out on the sand. The skimmers whined on the beach behind him. He looked around. The riders wore black masks that covered all but their mouths. Their cloaks

*billowed behind them as they sped toward him.
There was a humming sound in the air and Zeno
turned. In front of him a low, dark shape appeared.
Zeno sobbed with exhaustion.*

*"There it is!" he cried. "There's the tunnel. Go for it,
Prince! Leave me. I'm finished."*

*The dog turned and ran back, pulling on Zeno's
sleeve, barking fiercely.*

*"I can't," Zeno moaned as the humming sand skim-
mers grew ever closer.*

*Prince pulled harder until Zeno staggered to his
feet and limped toward the dark shape on the sand.
The Xarcons were only a few feet behind. Zeno looked
around as the leading rider drew a long, thin stick
from his belt. The stick flamed red as he raised it,
shimmering in the light reflected from the water.*

*Prince tugged at Zeno's pants leg as the boy stag-
gered, half blinded by the light stick, into the tunnel.*

"Yes!" shouted Emily, jumping to her feet. "They've
made it. They've gotten into the time tunnel! Look!
The Xarcons didn't catch them."

Neil Parker looked at his sister and smiled. Emily
was nine, two years younger than him. Her dark
brown hair was ruffled. Emily had a habit of running
her hands through her hair when she was excited.
And Emily *always* got excited when she watched *The
Time Travelers* on TV.

"Zeno and Prince always get away," said Neil above the program's closing theme music.

Emily shook her head. "So far," she said. "I thought they'd had it that time."

Mrs. Parker reached out and switched the TV off. "I'm surprised that show doesn't give you nightmares, Emily."

Emily grinned. "It's my favorite," she replied. Then she looked thoughtful. "I wonder where they'll get to next week."

"Somewhere weird and wonderful?" pondered Mrs. Parker, smiling.

"The time travelers *always* go to weird and wonderful places!" Neil rolled his eyes.

"You like *The Time Travelers* as well," said Emily accusingly. "You watch it, too."

"I wouldn't let Fudge see it," said Sarah, trying to hum the complicated theme music. "It's scary!"

Sarah was five. She had a hamster named Fudge and treated the little animal as if it were a person. Sarah was always telling people what Fudge thought of everything.

"It's Prince that I like," Neil said. "That dog can do tons of tricks." Neil gave Sam's ears a rub, and the pet black-and-white Border collie put his head on Neil's knee. "Do you think I could train Sam to be a TV star?"

Mrs. Parker laughed and tilted her head. "How about training yourself to do some homework?"

Neil grinned. "I promised Dad I would give him a hand in the kennel."

"What's that?" said a voice from the door. "Did I hear somebody say 'help'?"

Bob Parker was a tall man with thick dark hair and an infectious smile.

"Oh, Dad, *The Time Travelers* was great tonight," said Emily enthusiastically. "You should have seen it. Zeno and Prince ended up on this really weird planet and the Xarcons tried to capture them."

"But they got away just in time," said Mr. Parker.

"How did you know?" said Sarah.

"Magic!" said Mr. Parker.

Sarah's eyes grew round. "Wow! You're clever, Dad. I never know what's going to happen to Prince and Zeno."

Mrs. Parker picked up the newspaper. "That reminds me," she said, shuffling through the pages. "There's something in today's paper about your TV show, Emily."

Emily jumped up. "What was that?"

"Here it is."

Emily took the paper from her mother. "Oh, wow! Listen to this, Neil. *Popular children's TV series* The Time Travelers *is out on location in the Northwest area. The series follows the adventures of a boy and his dog who accidentally get sucked into a space-time tunnel and can't find their way home. Children all over the country follow their adventures every week*

as they travel backward and forward in time and space. So, watch out! They could be recording an episode of the new series somewhere near you!"

"Maybe they'll do an episode at a boarding kennel." Neil winked at his father.

"Now, what kennel do you have in mind?" Mr. Parker said, raising an eyebrow.

Mr. and Mrs. Parker ran King Street Kennels and rescue center. The whole family was crazy about dogs. They had a dark green Range Rover with the kennel's logo on the side and they were nicknamed the "Puppy Patrol" by everybody around Compton, the busy market town near where they lived.

"If they did an episode at King Street Kennels, Fudge could be in it," Sarah said.

"As if!" mocked Emily. She looked dreamy. "Wouldn't it be great, though?"

"I know one thing," Mr. Parker said. "I could do with a time tunnel right now."

"Why?" asked Emily.

"So I could go back a couple of hours and have time for all this work I have to do."

"I was just coming to help." Neil got up from his chair.

"I'll help, too," volunteered Emily.

"Promise me you'll do your homework later," Carole Parker insisted.

Neil laughed. "I promise! Come on, Dad, Emily and I are as good as a time tunnel. We'll get the work done in no time."

Bob Parker looked at his older daughter. She was still sitting cross-legged on the floor, her chin in her hands, lost in thought.

"Are you coming, Emily?" he asked.

Emily jumped. "Sorry, Dad. I was just thinking."

"Think outside with a bucket and mop." Mr. Parker chuckled.

"Come on, Sam," Neil called.

The Border collie sprang up at the sound of Neil's

voice. Sam had been found abandoned as a puppy when Neil was seven. The thin, frightened little dog had been brought to the rescue center and the Parkers adopted him as the family pet. Sam had been by Neil's side ever since and he was now fit and healthy. Neil had even taught him lots of agility skills so that he could enter competitions at county shows.

"We had an interesting new arrival today," Bob Parker said as he, Neil, and Emily made their way across the courtyard to one of the kennel blocks. Sam ran ahead, tail wagging. He loved visiting the other dogs.

"What breed?" Neil was always interested in new arrivals at King Street.

"It's an Irish wolfhound," Mr. Parker said. "His name is Fred and he is absolutely enormous."

"Wow!" said Emily. "We've never had an Irish wolfhound before."

A girl with fair hair tied back in a ponytail came out of the kennel block as they arrived. Sam raced up to her, tail wagging furiously.

"Hey, Sam!" the girl said. "That tail will fall off if you wag it so hard."

"Hi, Kate!" said Neil. "We're just going to have a look at Fred."

Kate McGuire was the King Street kennel assistant. She had no animals of her own, but she looked on all the dogs at King Street as her adopted pets.

Kate laughed. "Fred!" she said. "He should be called Giant or Monster or Mr. Enormous — not *Fred*."

"He isn't badly behaved, is he?" asked Emily.

Kate shook her head. "Not at all," she replied. "He's terrific — a real gentle giant. I've just been walking him — or rather, he's been walking me!"

Neil grinned. Kate could do anything with dogs. Even the most boisterous dogs calmed down when she was around.

"I'm off," she said, bending down to give Sam a pat. "See you tomorrow."

Neil waved as Kate got on her bike and rode off. He followed Emily and his dad into the kennel block.

There were two kennel blocks, one on either side of the courtyard. Each contained two rows of ten kennels with a passageway down the middle. Each pen had a basket for the dog to sleep in and a gate to an outside run.

Neil stopped to say hello to some of the dogs. There was a boxer and a Skye terrier in adjoining pens. They both rushed to greet Neil and Sam.

Farther down the row, Daisy looked up and yipped as Neil appeared. Daisy was a little dachshund that Neil had grown very fond of.

"Hi, Daisy," he said, stopping at her pen.

The dachshund waddled over and wagged her tail. Daisy was a little overweight. Neil knew that dachshunds got fat very easily and he had been very careful not to give her too many dog treats.

"Come and see Fred," Emily called from the far end of the row.

Neil hurried down toward the last pen, with Sam at his heels. He stood lost in admiration. Fred was magnificent.

"He's amazing!" Neil gasped.

Bob Parker lifted the latch and they went in. An enormous dog with a rough gray coat padded over to them and sniffed at Sam. Sam was dwarfed by the huge wolfhound.

"It's OK, Sam," Bob Parker said gently. "Fred won't eat you."

Sam lifted his muzzle and sniffed at the wolfhound. Then his tail began to wag again. Sam was used to getting along with lots of strange dogs.

"Hi, boy," Neil said, laying his hand on the wolfhound's back, which was level with Neil's waist. Fred looked up at him with liquid brown eyes.

"He's beautiful," Emily breathed.

"*Big* and beautiful is more like it," Mr. Parker said. "I had to give him an extra-large basket."

Neil ruffled the dog's ears and Fred nuzzled his hand in return.

"Why is he here, Dad?" Neil asked.

"His owner, Bill Grey, has gone away for a few days. We're going to have Fred until midweek."

"Great! I'll take him for a walk tomorrow."

"Hang on tightly," Mr. Parker warned. "He's a lot stronger than you."

"A wolfhound is a hunting breed, isn't it?" Neil asked.

Bob Parker nodded. "They were used to hunt stags hundreds of years ago. They were also called war hounds because kings and princes would ride into battle with them."

"You mean like knights in armor?" asked Emily, impressed.

"That sort of thing," said Bob Parker.

"I don't suppose Fred's owner is a king or a prince?" asked Emily.

Mr. Parker laughed. "Fred's owner has a butcher's shop in Padsham. Just as well, the way Fred eats!"

"Oh, well, at least Fred is staying at *King* Street," said Neil.

Mr. Parker pointed at some buckets nearby. "Come on — time to get to work with those mops."

Neil and Emily helped Mr. Parker mop out the kennels and make sure the water bowls were full.

"You two have been a great help," said Bob Parker as they finished. "Now I'll have time for a cup of coffee before class tonight."

There were dog training classes at King Street Kennels on Wednesday evenings and Sunday mornings. Bob Parker taught all the dogs in the area who needed a little extra help to behave properly. The noisy classes were held in the barn next to the kennel blocks.

"Can I help out?" asked Neil.

"I thought you had homework to do," said Mr. Parker.

Neil's face fell. "Oh, yeah. I forgot. I hate homework."

"You'd hate it even more if Mr. Hamley gave you detention," Emily said.

Neil grinned. Mr. Hamley was a teacher at Meadowbank School in Compton. He had a Dalmatian called Dotty and could be cool sometimes — but was *very* strict about schoolwork.

"Never mind. It's spring break next week," Mr. Parker reminded him.

"Thank goodness for that," said Emily. "No school for a whole week!"

"OK," said Neil. "I give in. I'll go and hit the books. I just hope Mr. Hamley realizes the sacrifice I'm making."

"He won't," said Emily.

Neil shook his head. "Homework! What's the point?"

CHAPTER TWO

"**T**he point *is*," said Mr. Hamley, "that you haven't done your homework, Barry, so you can't go to the audition until you *have* done it. You can do it at lunchtime, and if you finish it, *then* you might have time to catch the audition before it's over."

Barry Pringle's face fell. "I wish I *had* done it now," he said, shuffling past Neil.

Neil turned to his friend Hasheem.

"Wow! I'm glad I did *my* homework last night."

Hasheem shook his head. "Poor Barry," he said as the boy slouched back to his seat, head down. "He must be really disappointed."

Neil's class was buzzing with excitement after Mr. Hamley's announcement. Prince Productions, the TV company that made *The Time Travelers*, was recording an episode in nearby Padsham — and they were looking for children to be involved in some of the crowd scenes. There were going to be auditions at lunchtime in *their* school hall.

"Can you believe it?" asked Hasheem, leaning across his desk toward Neil. "This could be the start of my movie career."

"Dream on!" said Neil. "You'll only be in the background. Even if you *do* get picked, nobody will recognize you."

"Says who?" said Hasheem. "Haven't you ever heard of the star of the show breaking his leg and suddenly, from out of nowhere, the director says — 'Hasheem! This is your big break!'"

"If you don't get on with your work, *you* won't be going to the auditions, either," said a voice.

Hasheem looked up. "Uh-oh! Sorry, Mr. Hamley," he muttered.

Neil bent over his workbook. It was really hard to concentrate. He kept thinking about the auditions. Imagine getting a part in *The Time Travelers*!

It seemed ages before lunchtime finally came. Neil bumped into his best friend, Chris Wilson, outside the school hall.

"Are you going to audition?" Neil asked Chris.

"You bet. I think everybody will want to."

Chris was right. The school hall was full. Neil,

Chris, and Hasheem crammed themselves in at the back. The headmaster was up on the stage with Mrs. Potter, the drama teacher. There were two men standing beside them. One was youngish and fair. The other was older, with receding dark hair, and he looked a bit nervous.

Slightly behind them was a dark-haired boy with a dog. Neil recognized the young star who played Zeno in *The Time Travelers*. He was about the same age as Neil but didn't look very happy. Neil could see the dog sitting quietly at the boy's feet.

"It's Prince!" he whispered, gazing at the golden cocker spaniel.

Prince sat watching all the people in the hall with interest. He didn't seem the least bit bothered by the noise. The spaniel had silky ears, furry feet, and a long feathery tail. To Neil's expert eye, he was a perfect specimen of his breed.

"Attention, please!" said the headmaster, and the pupils fell silent.

"I want to introduce Mr. Mason, Mr. Jenkins, and Max," the headmaster went on. "They've come along this morning to audition potential supporting *artistes* for an episode of *The Time Travelers* that they'll be filming this weekend.

"*Supporting artistes?*" asked Hasheem, looking confused.

"'Extras' to you," whispered Chris.

"Now, I know you are all interested," continued the headmaster, "so let's hear more about it, shall we?"

He stepped aside and the fair-haired man walked forward.

"Hello, everybody. I'm Brian Mason, the director of the show. That means I'm responsible for what you see on your TV screens when you watch *The Time Travelers*. I deal with the filming of the show and also the casting of the characters. That's why I'm here today. I thought it would also be a good idea to bring along Mr. Jenkins, Max, and, of course, Prince. You'll be seeing them all again on Saturday if you are lucky enough to be chosen.

"The episode we'll be filming is set in medieval times and I'm looking for some people to be in the large crowd scenes we have planned."

"Wow! Knights in armor!" Chris said. "Do you think they'll give us swords?"

"We're going to be shooting mainly around Padsham Castle," Brian Mason went on. "The story is that Zeno and Prince help the rightful owner of the castle to get it back from his evil brother. Padsham is perfect for us, so we need people who can get there easily."

"Excellent," whispered Neil to Hasheem. "The castle is just a bike ride away."

"We also need people who've got a lot of patience," said Mr. Mason, smiling. "You probably won't believe me, but filming TV shows is mostly about standing around — and all too often when we're taping out-side, it means standing around in the rain."

"Patience?" said Chris. "That rules you out, Ha-sheem."

Mr. Mason spoke again. "One more thing. If you're chosen as an extra you'll need to make sure an adult can come to the set with you. If we use anybody un-der the age of sixteen we need a chaperone to be offi-cially responsible for them at all times. It's the law, I'm afraid."

"A chaperone!" said Hasheem. "What about my reputation?"

"You'll have to put up with it," said Chris. "You heard what the man said."

"It's for the sake of your art," said Neil, grinning.

Hasheem laughed. "Oh, well, in that case, I don't mind."

"Listen!" Neil whispered. "He's telling us what we have to do."

"We're going to ask you to walk around the room first," Brian Mason went on. "If I tap you on the shoul-der, please go to the side of the room and stay there."

"That's all?" said Chris. "It doesn't sound like much of an audition."

"Tut, tut. Have *patience*," said Hasheem, and Chris gave him a thump.

"Look! There's Barry," said Neil. "He must have done that homework in double-quick time."

Barry waved at them. His face was flushed and his hair stood on end.

"Made it!" he gasped as he came to stand beside them.

Mrs. Potter stepped forward and clapped her hands. "Just start walking around. Be yourselves — act natural."

Neil and Chris looked at each other. "OK, so we walk," said Neil as the whole crowd moved forward.

"I feel like an idiot," grumbled Chris.

"That's what Mrs. Potter said," Hasheem chipped in. "Just act normal."

The director jumped down from the stage and began to walk among them. Neil was still watching Prince. The man named Jenkins turned around to say something to Max and the dog flinched and shrank back. Max looked down, his hand going to Prince's head. The dog settled down, but Neil saw the boy's face tighten as he replied to Mr. Jenkins.

Neil felt a tap on his shoulder and turned in time to see Brian Mason heading off into the crowd. Neil walked toward the side of the room, head down. Emily and her friend Julie Baker were there already.

"So, you got the elbow, too?" said Emily gloomily.

Neil nodded and leaned back against the wall. "I was watching Prince," he sighed, kicking the wall with his heel. "I should have concentrated on walking."

"I'm sorry you lost out, too, Neil." Julie looked as

sad as he felt. Then she brightened a little as she gazed across the hall. "Isn't Prince gorgeous, though? He reminds me of Ben."

Ben was Julie's Old English sheepdog.

"How can he remind you of Ben?" Neil asked, amazed. "They're completely different breeds!"

"I know what Julie means." Emily looked thoughtful. "Prince is so friendly looking, just like Ben." She frowned. "I'd have loved to have been chosen."

Neil forgot his own disappointment and tried to cheer her up. "Never mind. At least you've seen Prince. And we can always go and watch."

Emily smiled. "Do you think Max would give me his autograph?"

Neil looked at the boy on the stage. He had his hand on Prince's neck. "Why not?" he said. "He seems all right — not too stuck-up or anything. He looks as if he likes Prince."

Hasheem and Chris came wandering up.

"There goes my movie career," said Hasheem. "Maybe I should have done one of my funny walks."

"Barry is still in the running," Neil said. "Lucky old Barry!"

"They must need an awful lot of extras," Chris said. "Look! Mr. Mason has finished eliminating people."

Neil looked around. There were about twenty boys and girls lining the walls.

"What did we do that was so bad?" groaned Hasheem. "I learned to walk years ago. I thought I was pretty good at it."

Mrs. Potter clapped her hands for silence.

"Thank you all so much," she said. "If the people at the side of the room could just stay there, Mr. Mason has some more selecting to do. The rest of you can go — I do hope you aren't too disappointed at not being picked."

Neil's mouth dropped open.

"*Yes!*" said Hasheem, punching the air. "We *were* selected."

They watched as everybody else filed out of the hall.

"Tough luck, Barry," Neil said as the other boy passed him.

Barry grinned. "At least I got to try."

Brian Mason smiled at the students who were left.

"Now I want to try a few things with you," he said. "I'm going to give you instructions and I want you to obey them as well as you can."

They had to do all sorts of things — team up in twos and in fives, run the length of the hall, fall down, jump up, cheer, and best of all, pretend they were attacking a castle wall.

"Great!" said the director from the stage when they had finished shouting battle cries at the top of their voices. "There's a scene in the episode where the local peasants join forces with Zeno and Prince and attack the castle. That looked terrific."

"Peasants," said Chris softly. "No chance of swords then?"

"Mrs. Potter and I have made some notes," the director went on. "We'll need fifteen extras from this group and the names will go up on the bulletin board this afternoon. Thank you all very much for coming."

"I can't stand the suspense," said Hasheem. "I won't be able to work at all this afternoon."

"So what's new?" said Neil, grinning.

Emily was almost dancing beside him. "I'm going to ask for Max's autograph," she said, pulling a piece of paper and a pencil out of her pocket.

Neil watched as Brian Mason and Mrs. Potter came down the steps from the stage, chatting together. Max was behind them with Prince.

"Excuse me," Emily said shyly, holding out the pencil and paper. "Can I have your autograph?"

Max looked around and smiled. "Sure," he said. "What do you want me to write?"

Emily and Max went into a huddle. Neil could hear Emily dictating a message to Max. Neil bent down and held out his hand, palm face up, to Prince. The cocker spaniel sniffed delicately, then licked his hand.

Neil smiled and crouched down, stroking Prince's silky coat, tickling him under the chin. Prince's eyes closed and he held his head up for more.

"What do you think you're doing?" said a voice.

Neil looked up. It was Mr. Jenkins.

"I was just saying hello," Neil replied.

The man grunted. "That's a valuable dog. Don't you go getting him upset. We can't have all you kids annoying him."

Neil flushed. "I wouldn't annoy him," he muttered. "And he *isn't* upset."

"What do you call that then, eh?" said Jenkins, pointing at the dog.

Neil looked down. Prince had backed off and Neil thought he was cowering a little.

"He was OK a moment ago," Neil said, surprised.

Mr. Jenkins grunted again. "Temperamental, that's what he is. He's spoiled rotten, that dog."

The man stomped away, tugging Prince's leash.

The dog followed him warily. Neil looked around and saw Max staring after him, his eyes stormy.

"I didn't do anything," Neil said, bewildered.

Max looked at him. For a moment Neil thought he was going to say something. Then he turned away and walked after the others.

"Well!" said Hasheem. "That wasn't very friendly, was it?"

"And he was so nice about the autograph," Emily commented. "I wonder what annoyed him."

Julie frowned. "Maybe he didn't like you petting Prince."

Neil bit his lip. "As if I would do anything to upset a dog."

Emily put her hand on his arm. "We know you wouldn't," she said. "But strangers might not realize that. Cheer up, Neil. If you get chosen as an extra you'll be able to show Max you aren't like that."

"*If,*" said Neil. "From the way Max looked at me, I don't think he would want me anywhere near him or Prince."

CHAPTER THREE

Neil, Chris, and Hasheem hurried out of class at the end of the lesson but Emily was still at the bulletin board before them.

"We're in!" she yelled, her face shining.

"What? All of us?" Chris couldn't believe it.

Julie clenched her fist. "Me, too! I'm so excited. Isn't it great?"

Neil looked at the list. It really *was* true. His name *was* there.

"We've got to be at Padsham Castle on Saturday morning at seven o'clock," he said, reading the notice. "They'll need us on Sunday, too."

"Seven!" groaned Hasheem. "That's the middle of the night!"

"It also says breakfast and lunch will be provided," Neil went on.

Hasheem looked a bit more cheerful.

"I'm really excited," laughed Emily, dancing around. "Just think! We'll be on TV. Do you think we'll get costumes?"

"We'll need to get an adult to come with us," Julie reminded them.

"I'll ask Mom," Neil said.

Hasheem pulled a notebook out of his bag and started scribbling in it.

"What are you doing?" Julie asked.

Hasheem looked surprised. "Practicing my autograph, of course!"

Chris gave him a shove. "Don't be silly. We're only extras."

"Everybody has to start somewhere," Hasheem said seriously. "This could be my big break."

Chris laughed. "Oh, sure. *Hasheem, star of stage and screen.*"

"It's going to be great seeing Prince at work," said Neil as they made their way out of school. "He's a really clever dog. Very well trained. Nothing seemed to bother him in school today."

"Except that Jenkins man," Chris chipped in.

Neil agreed. He suspected there was something more to Jenkins's aggressive manner than a lack of personality, but he couldn't figure out what.

Emily interrupted his thoughts. "Just wait till we tell Mom and Dad we're going to be on TV!"

"I can't wait till Saturday," Hasheem whooped as they were all swept out of the school gates by the rush of people. "Fame and fortune, here I come!"

"Look at all the people!" Neil said breathlessly as Mrs. Parker drove the Range Rover through the gates of Padsham Castle on Saturday morning. She wiped her brow with one hand. It was very hot.

"Where's Prince?" Sarah piped up.

"Inside, somewhere cool, if he has any sense," Emily said.

Even though it was so early in the morning, the whole lawn in front of the castle was already crowded with people. Some of them were running around with pieces of paper and complicated-looking equipment. Everyone seemed hot and sweaty. There were also a number of big blue trailers parked in the castle grounds with PRINCE PRODUCTIONS written on the side. The air felt close and sticky.

"I'd love a cool drink," said Neil.

Emily nodded. The heat had been building up all week and some of the dogs at King Street had been restless because of it.

"That looks like a catering trailer over there," said Emily. "Maybe we could buy some drinks."

Mrs. Parker maneuvered the Range Rover into a

parking space. "Where did you say you would meet the others?" she asked.

"By the drawbridge," Emily replied. "It's really great of you to chaperone us, Mom."

Carole Parker laughed. "As if I had any choice once Sarah heard about it!"

Sarah jiggled up and down in her seat. "I wish *I* could be an extra."

"You're too young," said Mrs. Parker. "But to make up for it, I'll buy you a drink, too. Come on. We'll meet you at the drawbridge, Neil."

Neil and Emily wove their way through the crowds.

"There's Mrs. Jones," said Emily, waving at a gray-haired lady with a dog who was standing by the drawbridge in front of the castle. "I bet she's thrilled by all this excitement!"

Mrs. Jones waved back and Toby, her little wire-haired terrier, barked a welcome. Toby was ten and came to King Street to board from time to time. He was a very lively little dog for his age and always up to mischief.

Neil sighed. "I wish I had been able to bring Sam. I feel really bad about leaving him behind."

"He's got all the other dogs at King Street to keep him company," Emily said. "Oh, look, Neil! Doesn't the castle look amazing?"

Padsham Castle wasn't really that old. It had been

built about a hundred years ago by an eccentric but very rich local man who thought it would be a good idea to live in a castle. But it *looked* really old — apart from the fact that it was in pretty good condition. It had turrets and slit windows and even a drawbridge in front of the huge main door.

The castle had been turned into a local history museum and Meadowbank School sometimes went on trips there. Maggie Jones lived in a cottage on the grounds. She was the caretaker and sold tickets for the museum, and kept an eye on the place.

"These people can't *all* be extras," said Emily, looking around in amazement.

Neil shook his head. "I bet a lot of people have come to watch." He smiled. "There's Chris!"

Chris was walking toward Mrs. Jones. Toby jumped up at him with a stick in his mouth.

Neil laughed. "Poor Toby, Mrs. Jones hasn't got time to play with him today."

"Lots of people have come to watch the show being made, haven't they?" Chris asked, eagerly looking around. "Mrs. Jones says she's never had so many visitors to the castle."

"It's true," Mrs. Jones said. "Twenty years I've been caretaker here and I've never seen it like this. And the trailers! Huge things parked all over the place. Wires trailing everywhere, people shouting, cameras. They've even got a mobile canteen!"

"We saw it," said Neil. "Mom's already gone to get us some drinks."

"It's so hot," Emily groaned.

"Certainly is," said Chris. "I could do with a drink, too. See you in a few minutes." He walked off in the direction of the catering trailer.

Mrs. Jones looked up at the sky. "This glorious weather has to break soon. Toby has been very jumpy these last few days."

"So have some of the dogs at King Street," Neil agreed. "One was spinning around in circles trying to catch her own tail! I think she was a bit uncomfortable in the heat." He bent down to Toby. "Poor Toby! How are you coping, boy?"

The little wirehaired terrier wagged his stumpy tail and dropped his stick at Neil's feet.

"OK," Neil said. "I'll throw it for you."

He picked up the stick and looked around. "There's a clear space over by the castle wall. Is it all right if I give Toby a quick run, Mrs. Jones?"

Mrs. Jones looked relieved. "That would be nice of you," she said, unclipping Toby's leash. "I've been so busy this morning I haven't had time — he loves chasing sticks."

"Come on, Toby," Neil called, breaking into a run.

Toby barked excitedly and chased after him across the castle drive. Out of the corner of his eye Neil saw a long black car sweep in through the gates of

the castle. There was an excited babble of voices from the crowd at the gates. Toby barked and Neil laughed.

"OK," he said. "Don't worry. I haven't forgotten our game."

He threw the stick and the little dog raced after it. Just at that moment the black car stopped at the drawbridge and Max got out, followed by Mr. Jenkins. Then Prince jumped out of the car.

Toby raced back to Neil with the stick, and Neil threw it toward the car. It was too late before Neil realized what he had done. Suddenly, Prince was off, racing toward the stick. Toby stopped, barked, and raced on.

"Prince!" Max shouted. "Come back!"

Mr. Jenkins swung around and saw Neil.

"Get that dog out of here!" he yelled.

Neil gulped. Toby was almost on the stick — so was Prince. Prince got to it first and raced off with it. Toby, barking excitedly, followed at his heels. Prince turned briefly, swerved, and scampered off in the other direction — toward Neil. Mr. Jenkins started running toward him, too, shouting as he went.

Neil made a dive for Prince as the dog hurtled past him, but Prince was too quick. The golden cocker spaniel swerved, his long feathery tail flowing behind him, just as Toby caught up. Neil found himself clutching Toby instead of Prince. He grabbed hold of Toby's collar and hung on. Then he gathered up the little dog into his arms.

"One down, one to go," he said.

"I'll get Prince," someone shouted, and Neil spun around.

Max was racing across the lawn toward the cocker spaniel, cornering him in a nook of the castle wall. Prince stopped and turned, looking at Max.

"Here, boy," Max said softly. "Give me the stick."

Prince began to walk toward Max, tail wagging.

"What the devil do you think you're doing?" roared a voice in Neil's ear. Neil felt Toby quiver in his arms.

Then he saw a flash of golden fur and Prince was off again.

Max whirled around. "You've scared him!" he said, angrily.

"Nonsense," said Mr. Jenkins. "He just can't behave properly."

Max bit his lip. Neil could see he was really upset. "He does what *I* tell him," Max muttered.

"That's because you're always giving him treats," said Jenkins. "What he needs is a bit of discipline."

"Don't you touch him," Max said through gritted teeth.

"I'm his trainer," retorted the man. "I should know."

Max looked furious. "If you lay a finger on him, I'll tell Brian."

Mr. Jenkins hesitated and his eyes shifted nervously. "Who said anything about laying a finger on him? Don't you go telling stories you can't prove. And if you're so good with him, you get him back."

Neil watched as Mr. Jenkins turned on his heel and walked off. "Wow!" he said to Max. "Is that *really* Prince's trainer?"

Max put his fingers between his lips and whistled. There was a rustle from a clump of bushes and Prince appeared, the stick still in his mouth. Max kneeled down, arms out, and Prince began to race toward him.

"It's his *temporary* trainer," Max said. "The real

one is sick and she won't be coming back for another two weeks."

Toby squirmed in Neil's arms, but Neil held on tight. "Oh no you don't," he told the little dog. "We've already got Max and Prince into enough trouble."

Max turned briefly and smiled. "It wasn't your fault. Jenkins doesn't like Prince. Sometimes you'd think he doesn't even like dogs!"

"Then why is he a dog trainer?" Neil asked.

Max didn't reply. Prince came galloping up and threw himself at the boy. Boy and dog fell in a heap, rolling over and over on the grass. The stick was forgotten as Prince and Max greeted each other. Jenkins might not like Prince very much, but one thing was certain. Max did. Max loved Prince.

CHAPTER FOUR

"**N**eil!" Chris yelled, running up with his hands full of cans of Coke. "They want us over at the costume trailer."

Julie and Hasheem were close behind him. They had drinks, too.

"Your mom and Sarah are coming," Julie said to Emily. "Hi, Mrs. Jones."

"We didn't even have to pay for the Coke!" said Hasheem, astonished. "I really like this acting thing."

"Look what I found," said Julie excitedly, waving a stack of colored papers in the air.

"It's a script," Neil marveled. "Let's take a look."

They all peered over Julie's shoulder as she leafed through the script.

"Baron Dredmore is the bad guy," said Julie. "He

takes over Sir Gareth Norton's castle — that's his brother — and Zeno and Prince arrive through the time tunnel. Then Baron Dredmore captures Prince."

"What happens then?" asked Hasheem.

Julie flipped through another few pages. "Oh, this is where we come in. Zeno gets all the villagers organized to storm the castle and rescue Prince and Lady Genevieve."

"Who's she?" asked Hasheem.

"Baron Dredmore has locked her in the tower," said Julie. "I think she's Sir Gareth's girlfriend."

"Knights didn't have girlfriends in those days," Emily said.

"So what did they have?" Julie asked.

Emily shrugged. "Something a lot more elegant than girlfriends."

"Never mind that," said Chris hurriedly. "We've got to go and get ready."

He pointed at one of the big blue trailers parked in a roped-off area just inside the castle walls. Several men in jeans and T-shirts were carrying cameras and light stands across the lawn and into the castle. Another two were herding a lot of spectators behind another roped-off area, well out of the way of the equipment, ready to start filming.

Carole Parker and Sarah arrived just as Neil handed Toby back to Mrs. Jones.

"Why don't you come over to the cottage for a cup of tea?" Mrs. Jones said to Carole Parker.

"I'd love that, Maggie," Mrs. Parker said.

"And I can play with Toby!" Sarah looked excitedly at the little dog.

"If you need me, you'll know where I am," Mrs. Parker told Neil.

Neil nodded. "See you later." Toby barked and Neil laughed. "You, too, Toby."

"Good luck," said Mrs. Jones. "What is it they say to actors? Break a leg!"

Julie snapped the ring-pull of her can and took a long drink. Her bangs were sticking to her forehead with the heat.

"That's better," she gasped. "I'm *so* hot! And we've still got to get costumes. I hope they aren't too heavy."

Emily began to drag Neil toward the castle gates. "And there's makeup. Mine will definitely run with this heat."

Neil looked at the trailer with interest as they approached. A side door was open and inside was a bar with costumes hanging from it. A worried-looking woman with unkempt hair and glasses on the end of her nose was lining up the extras.

"That must be the wardrobe director," said Julie. "Isn't it exciting?"

"Smallest in front," the wardrobe director told them. "Now, let me see, I want eleven peasants, one page boy, two milkmaids, and a shepherd's boy."

"Does the shepherd's boy have a dog?" Neil asked before he could help himself.

The woman looked at him over the top of her glasses. "No, but you'll do. Here's your costume. You'll get a shepherd's crook over there." She took a hanger with a pair of baggy pants, a loose shirt, and a leather jerkin off the bar and handed it to Neil.

"Poor you!" said Chris. "That jerkin looks heavy."

Neil sighed. "Where do I change?" he asked.

The woman looked at his jeans and T-shirt. "There's a trailer for all the extras to change in," she said. "But your costume will easily go on over the clothes you're wearing, if you like."

"No way! I'd rather take them off, thank you. I'm boiling."

"No star dressing room for you," Hasheem joked.

The woman grabbed him. "You'll make a great page boy," she said. "Here, put these on."

Hasheem looked in disbelief at the short tunic, the leggings, and the hat with a feather in it.

"I can't wear *that*," he said, in disgust.

"You want to be on TV, don't you?" the woman said, her hands on her hips.

Hasheem nodded.

"Then that's what you wear. Next!"

Chris was still hooting with laughter at Hasheem when the woman grabbed him. "You're a peasant," she announced briskly.

"Thanks a lot." Chris sighed, taking a heap of what looked like rags from her.

When Hasheem and Chris came out of the extras' dressing trailer, Neil was already at Makeup. His costume fit perfectly.

The makeup girl slapped some cream on his face and rubbed it in. Then she dipped her fingers in a pot

of gray gook and spread some over his hands and face.

"Yuck!" said Neil. "What's that for?"

"To make you look as if you haven't washed for a week," the girl said, smiling. "Boys in the Middle Ages didn't have showers, you know."

"What I want to know," said Emily, coming over to them, "is why couldn't I be a princess instead of a peasant?"

Julie was with her. She had a white apron over a long blue dress and she was carrying a wooden bucket.

Neil looked her up and down. "You don't look too bad."

Julie grimaced. "I'm a milkmaid."

"You're lucky then," said the makeup girl. "You don't have to look dirty. Line up over there and you'll get your instructions."

"Over there" was in front of the drawbridge, far away from the spectators. A crowd of people had gathered around the edge of the roped-off area, pointing and smiling at the actors.

Emily joined Neil and the others, looking excited. "We just saw Max. He has a chaperone all to himself."

"She's named Suzie and she has to be on set when Max is working," added Julie. "She's really nice."

"Look, there she is, going into the castle with Max," Emily said, pointing.

Neil looked. Max was with a tall, dark-haired

woman. She and Max looked as if they were sharing a joke.

Brian Mason was standing on the drawbridge with a youngish-looking man who had bright red hair and wore gold-rimmed glasses.

"Gather 'round," Brian said to the extras.

Everybody shuffled into place while Brian introduced the man beside him.

"This is Jeff Calton. He's the producer of the series and he's always doing ten things at once! Jeff's going to quickly explain what we want you to do today."

Jeff peered at the group through his glasses and smiled. "You all look great. And I know you're going to do your best for us and for *The Time Travelers*. I hope you're all fans."

Everybody nodded.

"Great," Jeff went on. "I'm the guy in charge of this whole operation here today, and it's important that everything goes without a hitch. We always like to use fans as extras because they take their work seriously. If there are any problems, let me know at once. Problems cost time and money and the sooner we solve them, the better for everybody. Understood?"

There were more nods all around. Neil was impressed.

"Good," said Jeff. "Now, we're going to be doing all of the scenes set inside the castle today." He looked up at the sky. "It's a bit overcast for exterior shots, and besides, it'll be cooler inside."

Everybody sighed with relief. Neil looked up. The sky was already heavy with heat and the light wasn't very good.

Brian Mason took over and began to describe how the first shot was going to work. "The first scene we're going to shoot this morning is just after Zeno creeps into the castle to rescue Prince, who has been kidnapped by Baron Dredmore. You are all helping him because you hate Baron Dredmore and want to restore the castle to its rightful owner, Sir Gareth Norton. Baron Dredmore catches Zeno, then Sir Gareth arrives and leads you all into the castle. We're going to shoot the scene from inside the great hall. We'll get a shot through the doorway of Sir Gareth jumping off his horse, so all you have to do is come in after him, waving your hands in the air and shouting." The director looked around his cast of young villagers. "Any questions?"

"What do we shout?" asked Emily.

Jeff Calton smiled. "Let's leave that to your imagination and see how it goes. But nothing rude."

"Let's try it a couple of times before we go for a take," Brian said, giving a signal to the production crew behind them.

Neil grinned. This was going to be great.

"Wow!" gasped Chris. "Look at that!"

Neil looked around. Max was walking toward them with two other actors and Prince. One of the actors was dressed all in black and looked really frightening. Neil knew that had to be Baron Dredmore. The other one was riding a beautiful chestnut horse with a kind of skirt under its saddle. He was carrying a shield and wearing armor and a helmet with a huge white plume on top of it. He must be Sir Gareth. There was a man wearing riding boots walking by the horse's side.

"I suppose that's the horse trainer," Emily guessed. "Don't the knights look terrific?"

Neil laughed. "Sir Gareth should have a Fred with him."

"What's a Fred?" said a voice behind him.

Neil looked round. It was Jeff. "Oh," Neil muttered, embarrassed. "Sorry! I didn't know you were there."

"So, what *is* a Fred?" Jeff asked again.

"Fred is a dog," Neil said. "Actually, he's an Irish wolfhound. He's staying at our kennel right now, and my dad was telling me that in the olden days kings and princes and barons and people like that used to have wolfhounds."

Jeff's eyes lit up behind his glasses. "A sort of war hound, then. Of course! I never thought of that."

"Places, everybody!" Brian shouted as Max and the two men crossed the drawbridge. "Let's get this show on the road."

* * *

Fifteen minutes later the cameras were ready to record the scene.

"This is great," Emily said as they trooped out of the castle for the third time. "But it's just as well they've cleared all the exhibits out of the great hall, with all of us rushing around."

"Not all of them," Julie pointed out. "They've still got that big chair in there. It looks like a throne now that it's all draped with velvet and stuff. It's really cool."

"I love all the shouting," Neil said. *"Down with Baron Dredmore!"*

"Poor Hasheem doesn't get to do any shouting," Chris said. "All he has to do is stand behind that throne thing."

Neil looked up at the sky. "At least he's out of the rain." The first drops were beginning to fall. "Maybe a good downpour will clear the air."

"OK, on my cue — *go*! And, remember, don't look at the camera," called the director from the drawbridge.

Sir Gareth trotted across the drawbridge on his horse, flung himself from the saddle, and ran into the castle. The villagers followed, shouting enthusiastically.

Neil burst through the castle door with Chris and Julie beside him. Max was standing in front of the huge chair, which had a red velvet cushion on it. Baron Dredmore had Prince by the collar in one hand and his sword in the other.

"No, you don't!" yelled Max, and made a lunge for Baron Dredmore's sword.

Baron Dredmore raised his sword — and Sir Gareth raced across the floor, knocking it from his hand. The crowd cheered. Baron Dredmore let go of Prince and turned to face Sir Gareth. Prince scampered off.

"Cut!" shouted Brian.

Neil looked around. "Look at Prince!"

The cocker spaniel was sitting on the big chair in the center of the hall, looking as if he belonged there.

"No wonder he's called Prince," Chris said, chuckling. "That chair really does look like a throne."

Max heard him and turned, laughing. Then Jenkins, the trainer, walked over to the chair and took hold of Prince's collar. Prince barked and refused to budge.

"He likes it there," Julie said, smiling.

Jenkins turned to her. "That dog is spoiled. He won't do a thing he's told."

Jeff Calton walked over, eager to get the proceedings started again as soon as possible. He took his glasses off and polished them on his T-shirt. He looked worried. "You aren't having trouble with him again, are you, Harry?"

Harry Jenkins pursed his lips. "The dog is temperamental. He's unmanageable sometimes."

Max moved forward. "No, he isn't. *You* just don't know how to handle him."

Jeff looked at Max. "I haven't got time for this, Max. I've told you about this before. Mr. Jenkins is the trainer around here. Let's not forget that, eh?" The producer looked stressed.

Max bit his lip. Neil felt really sorry for him. But, he thought, performing dogs had to do what the trainer told them. Maybe Prince *was* getting a bit unruly.

"I might have another job for you, Harry," Jeff told Jenkins. "I'm thinking about getting a wolfhound in on some of the scenes with Sir Gareth."

"A wolfhound!" grumbled Jenkins, shaking his head. "You'd better be careful there. Wolfhounds can be dangerous animals."

"Can they?" said Jeff, looking concerned. "I didn't know that. Maybe it isn't such a good idea after all." He looked around and smiled at Neil. "It *was* only an idea."

Neil's mouth dropped open in surprise.

"He took you seriously!" Chris whispered to him.

But Neil wasn't listening. Jenkins was looking at him and the expression on his face wasn't pleasant.

Neil's mind raced. Why was the trainer looking at him like that? Then he knew. Jenkins was angry because he realized Neil had suggested having a wolfhound in the show. Neil looked at the trainer.

What had he said about wolfhounds? That they were dangerous? Nonsense! Wolfhounds were the gentlest dogs you could find. But they *were* big. What was the matter with Jenkins? A dog trainer who was scared of dogs? Jeff seemed too busy to notice what was going on right in front of him. Neil shook his head. But what on earth *was* going on?

CHAPTER FIVE

"**Y**ou almost got a part in *The Time Travelers* today, Fred," Neil said to the Irish wolfhound later that evening.

"What's that?" asked Mr. Parker.

Neil was making the evening rounds of the kennels with his father, finishing up with Fred. He could hear the rain drumming on the roof. It had been raining steadily since late afternoon.

"The producer heard me saying that Sir Gareth should have a wolfhound," Neil explained. "He thought it was a great idea at first."

"But he changed his mind?" his dad asked.

Neil bent down and ruffled Fred's ears. The big dog put his paws on Neil's shoulders and wagged his tail.

"Mr. Jenkins, the trainer, said wolfhounds were too fierce." Neil looked into Fred's liquid eyes. "But that isn't true, is it, Fred? You're as soft as putty."

"It certainly isn't true," said Mr. Parker, puzzled. "What an odd thing for a trainer to say."

Neil shrugged. "Max says Mr. Jenkins doesn't like dogs. Is that weird or what?"

He stood up, dislodging Fred's paws. The wolfhound nuzzled Neil's hand.

Neil frowned. "The producer just doesn't see it, either. He's always too wrapped up in other things when he's on the set. I'd like to find out more."

"Time to go, anyway," Mr. Parker said.

Neil gave Fred a final pat and latched the door of the pen. He followed his father out of the kennel block.

"You know, Dad, Mr. Jenkins does seem a bit nervous — even around Prince."

Mr. Parker shook his head. "That's just about the worst thing to be when you're handling dogs. Unless Prince *has* shown signs of a bad temper. Has he ever snapped at anybody?"

Neil shook his head. "Not that I've seen. But Prince isn't very good at doing what Mr. Jenkins tells him."

"Mmm," said his dad thoughtfully. "It might just be that they don't get along."

"Maybe."

"You don't sound convinced."

"I'm not. And I'm going to keep an eye on Mr. Jenkins. I don't think it's Prince's fault that they don't get along — *if* that's what's wrong."

Bob Parker laughed. "You *never* blame the dog, Neil."

Neil laughed back. He felt better. "I wonder where I got *that* idea from!"

As they ran through the rain to the house, Neil thought of his dad's favorite saying — if a dog has a problem, look at the owner. Or, in this case, the trainer. Then another thought occurred to him. Who *was* Prince's owner?

Neil got a chance to ask that question the next morning back at the castle. Chris's mom was acting as chaperone that day and was having a great time looking around the set. Neil had a couple of minutes before he was needed on set and left the others to search for Max.

He found the young actor still in Makeup and peered into the trailer. "Hi, Max. I'm not disturbing you, am I?"

Max turned around in his seat in front of a large mirror and smiled. "No way. Come on in. Excuse me for not looking at you while we talk, though — I'm still getting the gook caked on!"

Neil clambered in and sat down on an upturned basket behind Max's chair. "It's nothing, really. I was just wondering about Prince."

"Great, isn't he? What about him?"

"Do you own him?"

Max sighed. "I wish he *were* my dog. Prince is from an agency. They supply the other animals we use, too. I suppose the agency owns him."

Neil studied Max for a moment. The young actor wasn't much different from himself. A bit taller, perhaps, and his hair was darker, but it was clear that, like him, Max loved dogs and was very attached to

Prince. Neil hoped he hadn't asked something that had upset him. "I wish he was yours, too," Neil said, nodding. "Prince does everything you tell him."

Their conversation was interrupted by a shout from just outside the doorway, "Places, everybody!" It was Brian Mason. "Let's try to get these outside shots done before the rain comes again. We've got a lot to do today."

"Come on, Max," said a voice behind Neil.

He looked around. It was Suzie, Max's chaperone. She smiled at Neil. "Enjoying yourself?" she asked.

Neil nodded enthusiastically. "It's great, thanks. We're all loving it."

Suzie smiled again and Neil watched her and Max walk off toward the first location. Mr. Jenkins might be a problem for Max, but Suzie was a definite bonus!

Neil followed them for a moment and then saw Mrs. Wilson again, standing behind one of the cameras, watching all the activity. He waved at her and she smiled back.

There weren't nearly so many spectators this morning. It had rained all night and the grass was wet and slippery underfoot. But the rain hadn't cleared the air. If anything, it was even muggier than the day before.

Clouds were starting to pile up on the horizon and the atmosphere felt hot and heavy. Thunder grumbled in the distance. The rain wouldn't hold off for long. Maybe another shower would cool the air down a little. Neil felt hot and sticky in his costume. He could see Mrs. Jones and Toby at the door of their cottage, trying to get some fresh air.

Neil went to his place by the drawbridge where the other extras were gathered. He greeted his friends and looked around him, still fascinated by the thrill of being part of an actual episode of *The Time Travelers*.

All the scenes filmed that day were going to be outside on the castle grounds. There were four cameras set up, with thick cables trailing everywhere. One of the cameras was on the drawbridge itself, two on the lawn, and one right on top of the battlements.

They were going to shoot the scene where Sir Gareth returned to his castle after years away. Neil looked up at the battlements. They would get a great aerial shot from there. Then he looked at Sir Gareth, waiting to ride into the scene. What a pity he didn't have a Fred with him! It would have looked magnificent. Max was behind Sir Gareth on a little gray pony, and Prince was sitting patiently on the grass looking up at Max.

"Let's hope that dog gets it right the first time," said a voice behind Neil. "It's going to rain soon."

Neil turned around. Mr. Jenkins was standing behind him, his eyes on Prince.

"How long have you been a trainer, Mr. Jenkins?"

Neil seized this unexpected opportunity to find out more about the man's strange behavior.

Jenkins looked suspicious. "What business is it of yours?"

Neil shrugged. "None, I suppose. Sorry, I'm very interested in dogs, that's all. You don't seem to like them very much."

"Is that so? I've been training dogs for ten years now," said Mr. Jenkins briskly, rubbing his hand along his arm.

Neil bit his lip. "Oh. It's just —"

"You've got to show them who's boss," Jenkins cut in abruptly, "otherwise you just set yourself up for a lot of trouble." It was obvious from the tone of his voice that he didn't want to discuss the matter further.

Neil watched as Mr. Jenkins turned and walked off.

"Quiet, everybody. Ready? Action!" shouted Brian.

Sir Gareth started his ride across the lawn. Neil snapped to attention and watched Max follow on his pony, with Prince trotting alongside. The extras turned to watch and point. Suddenly the grumbling thunder got louder. Neil saw Prince stop and turn back the way he had come. Sir Gareth's horse moved restlessly, pulling on the reins. Neil looked up. A great crack of lightning split the clouds and suddenly there was a loud roll of thunder.

"Cut!" shouted the director. "Will somebody get that dog out of the frame!"

Neil caught a flash of movement out of the corner of his eye. Toby had jumped out of Mrs. Jones's arms and was racing in terror across the lawn. Mrs. Jones ran after him.

"Toby!" she called. "Come back here!"

But her voice was lost in another crack of thunder as lightning forked across the sky.

"Get everything under covers," Jeff Calton yelled, racing for the nearest shelter.

The first heavy drops of rain started to fall. Mrs. Jones ran on, but by this time Toby was far ahead. Neil called the little dog's name. Sir Gareth's horse reared in terror as yet another flash of lightning lit the castle walls and thunder boomed from the battlements.

Toby was headed straight for the horse. Prince lunged forward and started to bark furiously at Toby, warning the little dog away. Toby stopped, confused, as Prince ran toward him. Then swerving, the little dog ran on toward the horse's flailing hoofs.

The rain began to fall in great driving sheets with stinging drops almost blinding Neil as he stood trying to watch. Toby was barking in a frenzy — nothing seemed to distract him.

Sir Gareth was still unaware of the impending danger and was having trouble controlling his horse, which shuffled and stamped its enormous shaggy hoofs.

"No, Toby!" Neil yelled, running toward Toby just as the little dog was almost under the horse's hoofs.

Neil looked up. Sir Gareth pulled hard on the reins to try to regain control of the animal. The horse swerved and Neil threw himself at Toby, gathering up the terrified dog into his arms. Prince scampered out of harm's way as Max leaped down from his pony and ran to him.

Rain washed over Neil, running down his face, into his eyes, soaking him. He turned as he heard Mrs. Jones cry out. She was stumbling blindly toward them.

"It's all right. I've got him," Neil called.

Mrs. Jones tried to stop, but her feet slipped on the wet grass and she fell heavily.

Sir Gareth leaped off his horse and seized the reins, trying to lead the frightened animal away, but it pulled against him, pawing at the ground. The horse trainer ran up and grabbed the reins, steadying the animal.

Someone rushed past Neil. It was Jeff. He kneeled down and cradled Mrs. Jones's head in his arms. The old lady looked very white and her eyes were closed. Her right leg was bent under her at an impossible angle.

"Is she badly hurt?" Neil gasped.

Jeff looked up, his face streaming with water. "She's fainted. I think her leg might be broken. Take care of the dog. I'll see to Mrs. Jones."

Brian ran up, a cell phone in his hand.

"I'll call an ambulance," he shouted.

Behind him was a man with a huge umbrella. He opened it and held it over Jeff and Mrs. Jones.

"Careful with that phone, Brian," Jeff said. "There's lightning around, remember."

Brian looked across the lawn to the open door of the cottage and thrust the cell phone back in his pocket. "I'll call from there. We'll try to get Mrs. Jones into the cottage if she can be moved." He ran off toward the house.

Mrs. Wilson appeared, her face showing concern. "Can I help?" she asked.

"Chris's mom is a nurse," Neil explained. "She's chaperoning us today."

In the distance, they heard the siren of the emergency medical technicians' vehicle.

"A nurse?" she said to Mrs. Wilson. "That's great."

Mrs. Wilson bent over Mrs. Jones, felt her pulse, and ran a hand gently over the twisted leg.

"I don't think it's safe to move her. We must be careful of that leg. We'll wait for the paramedics."

"OK. Everybody else into the castle," the wardrobe director told them briskly. "Come on, out of the rain. The costumes will be ruined."

Neil stood where he was for a moment, then he felt a tug on his arm.

It was Chris. "Come on, Neil. Mom will look after Mrs. Jones. Get Toby out of the rain!"

Neil looked down. The little dog was shivering violently in his arms.

"Sorry, Toby," he said as he followed Chris. "Let's get you inside. Where's Emily?"

"Already inside," Chris replied.

Neil looked back just as he reached the castle door. Toby was squirming in his arms, trying to get down, wanting his owner. Jeff and the EMT were shielding Mrs. Jones from the rain with umbrellas. Mrs. Wilson had covered her in blankets and looked as if she had everything under control.

"Not yet, Toby," Neil whispered, trying to calm the little animal. "You come with me. I'll look after you."

The great hall was full of people, standing in huddles, dripping water all over the floor. Neil saw Max taking some towels from one of the technicians and then looking around for the dogs.

"Bring Toby over here, Neil. I can dry Prince off with one of these. You can do the same."

Neil and Max pushed their way through the other actors and technicians toward the big chair in the middle of the hall. Chris left them to look for the others.

"Thanks," Neil said, taking one of the towels from Max's outstretched hand.

Neil and Max rubbed the dogs down until they were dry.

Neil looked at the cocker spaniel, still panting and enjoying all the attention from Max. "Prince is amaz-

ing. He was really excited by all the thunder and lightning, but he never really lost control, did he? I think he even enjoyed getting wet!"

Max smiled. "Nothing upsets Prince," he said. "He's got nerves of steel. I think he's used to all the bangs and flashes we put him through by now."

Toby was standing on the end of a table with his fur ruffled. He barked at Prince, wanting his new friend to play with him.

Max smiled. "What are you going to do with him?"

Neil frowned. He could hear the sound of an ambulance siren in the distance.

"I hadn't really thought about that," he said. "I suppose Mrs. Jones is on her way to the hospital." Then his face cleared. "But that's OK. I'll just take him home with me. He can stay at our kennel — he's been with us before."

"Kennel?" said Max.

"King Street Kennels, of course!" Chris Wilson appeared again beside him. "It's where Neil lives. The best hotel for dogs in Compton!"

Max opened his mouth to say something, but Neil had already turned away.

"I hope Mrs. Jones is going to be OK." Neil looked thoughtful.

"If she is, it'll be no thanks to that dog!"

Everyone turned to see Mr. Jenkins. Behind him, Jeff Calton was wiping his glasses on his wet shirt, trying to dry them off.

"What do you mean?" asked Max, hotly.

"It was Prince that started it." Mr. Jenkins was looking directly at Prince. "Why did he have to start barking like that? He scared the horse *and* that other dog."

Neil whirled round. "That isn't true. It was the thunder that scared the horse. If it hadn't been for Prince, Toby would have run right under the horse's hoofs."

Jenkins looked irritated. "So you say. But I know what I saw. And —"

"That's enough," said Jeff soothingly, running a hand through his hair. He looked at Neil. "Look, I know you caught Mrs. Jones's little dog. And I'm grateful to you. But Mr. Jenkins is the dog expert here."

Neil flushed. "Sorry," he mumbled. "But it wasn't the way Mr. Jenkins said."

"I said that's enough!" Jeff Calton's face was pale and he looked really worried. "This is all I needed right now. I'm off to the hospital to see how Mrs. Jones is. Brian will take care of things here. The plan was to finish up here today, but now we'll have to come back next week."

"Why can't we go on now?" asked Max.

Jeff frowned. "The place is a mire. The equipment is going to have to be checked when the weather eases off. And, of course, we didn't get today's scenes done."

"You could do them tomorrow. We'll still be available — it's our spring break." Chris was desperate not to lose the opportunity to be in *The Time Travelers*.

Jeff shook his head. "Unfortunately, tomorrow is a bank holiday and the castle is booked for two days. We *can* pick up what we need to, but it'll be Wednesday before we can start shooting again. That means finding accommodation for the people who will have to stay and look after the equipment, redress the set, repair the damage — all that stuff. The actors have a couple of days off. Rats. We'd intended to be finished with Padsham today."

"When will *you* be back?" Max asked anxiously.

"I'm going to Manchester after I've been to the hospital." Jeff Calton looked at Max. "Look, I know you like Prince, but this is getting out of hand. I'm going to see if I can get another dog."

Neil and Max were shocked.

"We've got several more episodes in the series to shoot," Jeff continued, "and I need a dog I can rely on. Things just aren't working out with Prince anymore, are they? I have to take Mr. Jenkins's word on this matter."

Jeff Calton turned on his heel and walked off. Jenkins grunted, then followed him. Neil turned to Max. The boy's face was white.

"It's not right," said Neil. "What Jenkins said wasn't true. Prince saved Toby's life."

Max buried his face in Prince's coat. "It's no good

CHAPTER SIX

"What? You're kidding, right?" Neil couldn't believe what he had just heard.

"I'm deadly serious." Max looked up. "I'm sick of being ignored."

Neil was shocked. He desperately thought about what he could do to make Max change his mind. He suddenly had a brilliant idea.

"I know somebody who will listen to us."

Max didn't react. "Who?" he asked flatly.

Neil smiled. "My dad."

"Lucky you," said Max. "But what good does that do me?"

Neil thought for a moment. "I don't know, but you could have a talk with my dad. I've already told him about Mr. Jenkins."

"Do you really think Jeff would change his mind?" asked Chris.

Neil shrugged. "He might. But what's important is Prince. If Dad got a look at Prince he would be able to tell us what he thinks about him being spoiled. He runs obedience classes and can tell if a dog needs discipline, like Mr. Jenkins says."

"Prince doesn't," Max said firmly, giving the spaniel's ears a quick scratch. "He's so cool. Anyone can see that."

"Sticking up for Prince again, Max?" Brian Mason said, coming up to them.

"He's a good dog, Brian."

The director looked at Max and shook his head. "He's been giving us a lot of trouble on set lately."

"And we all know why," Max mumbled under his breath.

"Anyway, now we've got another problem with him."

"What now?" asked Max impatiently.

"We're going to have to find a place for him to stay for the next few days."

Max's eyes suddenly lit up. "Neil's mom and dad run a boarding kennel in Compton."

Brian looked at Neil. "Really? Do you think they could take Prince for a while?"

"I *think* they could," Neil said slowly. "I mean, we've got room. But I'd have to call and ask them."

Brian dug into his pocket and brought out his cell

phone. "Go ahead. Tell them I'll bring Prince around right away if it's OK with them."

"When can we leave?" asked Max confidently.

Brian laughed. "*You'll* have to ask your chaperone, but I'm sure Suzie will let you. After all, we're finished here for the day, that's for sure." He shook his head. "I bet you'd be happy to spend the next few days in Prince's kennel with him, wouldn't you?"

Max laughed back at Brian. "I don't know about *in* the kennel, but I'd like to be *with* him." Suddenly he looked concerned. "Does this mean I can stay around, too?"

"Ask your parents. You are due to go home for a couple of days," Brian said, thinking. "But if you wanted to stay and Suzie is around, I suppose you could hang out here. A lot of the crew will be staying on."

"I'd like to stay. If Jeff gets a new dog I might never see Prince again. I'd like to be able to visit him at the kennels."

Neil looked at Max. The boy's hand was resting on Prince's head and his eyes looked as big and dark as the dog's. Max would really miss Prince. An idea began to form in Neil's mind.

Brian ran a hand through his hair. "And that's another thing I'll have to organize — accommodation for everybody." He looked at Neil. "If your parents could take Prince, it would be a load off my mind."

"I'll call right now," Neil said. He looked at the little dog sitting by his feet. "I was going to ask them to take Toby anyway."

Brian grinned. "You must have really understanding parents."

"Oh, I do," Neil agreed, grinning. "Especially when it comes to dogs."

"Tell them we'll come around whenever they want." Brian disappeared to begin organizing the crew.

Neil nodded and punched the office number on Brian's cell phone.

"Do you think they'll take Prince?" Max asked.

Neil nodded. "They've never refused a dog yet." Then he grinned. "And I have another idea."

"This sounds ominous!" Chris dug Max playfully in the ribs.

"What is it?" Max was anxious to find out.

"Wait and see," Neil laughed. Then he broke off. "Oh, hi, Mom. I've got a favor to ask."

"And these are the kennel blocks." Neil was leading the way across the courtyard at King Street Kennels. Brian, Suzie, and Max were being shown around by Neil and his father.

Max looked around. "This is terrific! You're so lucky to live here, Neil. You'd be happy here, wouldn't you, Prince?"

The cocker spaniel looked up at him and wagged

his tail. Toby trotted beside him. The little terrier had recovered from his fright.

"He'd have Toby for company," Bob Parker said. "Those two seem to get along really well."

"Oh, Dad, did Mom phone the hospital?" Neil asked.

Bob Parker nodded. "Mrs. Jones has had her leg set, but she'll be in the hospital for a couple of days, just to make sure everything is all right. I said I'd pop in later this evening."

"I'll visit, too," Brian Mason agreed. "I'll take her the biggest bunch of flowers I can find. I feel so guilty about her accident."

Neil was surprised. "It wasn't your fault. The grass was slippery from the rain."

"It's just that it happened on set," said Brian. "The company will pay for Toby's board as well as Prince's. That's the least we can do."

"I'm sure Mrs. Jones will appreciate that," said Bob Parker.

Brian smiled. "You're a lifesaver, Bob," he said. "Now all I've got to do is confirm accommodation for the humans who need to stay on. In most cases I think I'll be able to extend the existing bookings."

"What about me?" asked Max. "I'd still really like to stay with Prince. We've only got a few days left."

Suzie put an arm around his shoulder. "Poor Max. We'll visit every day if the Parkers think that's OK."

"Hang on. I had an idea about that," said Neil, tripping over his words in his hurry to get them out. "I spoke to my Mom and Dad about it when we got here. Max can stay with us if he wants. Then he'll be *really* close to Prince."

"Really?" Max's eyes were glowing. "With all these dogs? That would be so cool."

Bob Parker burst out laughing. "It'll mean bedding down in a sleeping bag on Neil's floor, but I don't suppose you'll mind that."

"You bet I won't. I'm not that stuck-up, you know!" He turned to Neil. "Cool!"

Neil nodded. "No problem."

"You'll need permission, Max," Suzie chipped in. "You'll have to see what your parents have to say about it."

"Oh, Suzie, Mom and Dad will let me stay here if you tell them it's OK," Max said. "They've already said I can stay down here until we start shooting again."

Suzie grinned. "I'm sure you're right!"

"So everybody's happy?" Brian looked relieved. "You must feel like Santa Claus, Bob."

Bob Parker grinned. "I've got an ulterior motive. I'm going to get Max to help out with the kennel work."

"Really?" said Max, eagerly. "When can I start?"

CHAPTER SEVEN

The next day, Mrs. Parker drove Max and Neil into Compton to see Mrs. Jones in the hospital. They had brought Toby and Prince along, too.

"Are you sure it's all right to take the dogs?" Max asked as they pulled up at the hospital.

Neil nodded. "The hospital has a pets visiting policy."

"I think it's a really good idea," Mrs. Parker agreed. "Children get so attached to their pets, especially dogs. They make a much better recovery if they can see them sometimes."

"Mrs. Jones is going to be so happy to see Toby," Neil said as he and Max clipped the leashes on the dogs.

Mrs. Jones *was* happy. Her face lit up as they

walked into the ward, and several of the other patients turned to admire the dogs.

Toby was straining at his leash to get to his owner but Neil kept a tight hold.

"Hang on to him, Neil," Mrs. Parker warned. "Pets visiting is one thing, but we can't have them running around!"

"So *this* is Toby," a nurse said as Toby reached Mrs. Jones. "I've heard so much about the little champ."

"Meet Nurse Williams," beamed Mrs. Jones. "She's been so good to me."

The old lady was sitting in a chair by her bed with her leg propped up on a stool. She was surrounded by flowers. One huge vase was crammed with blooms. Brian Mason hadn't been joking when he said he'd get the biggest bunch he could find.

"Isn't he wonderful?" Mrs. Jones looked so happy as Mrs. Parker handed Toby to her. Toby's short stubby tail was waving madly as he reached up to lick Mrs. Jones's face.

Mrs. Jones's eyes were bright. "It's such a comfort to know he's at King Street."

"He loves it there," said Neil. "But I think he'd rather be with you."

Mrs. Jones laughed as Toby tried to climb all over her.

"And there's Prince!" She reached down to stroke the cocker spaniel. "It was very thoughtful of you to

bring him to see me, Max. I hear you've had to stop
filming *The Time Travelers* because of the storm."

A sudden flash of recognition crossed the nurse's
face.

"I wondered where I'd seen you before. The children

always gather around the TV when *The Time Travelers* is on. They think you're great — and Prince, too!"

Max blushed. "Prince is the real star of the show."

Nurse Williams glanced around toward the children's wing. "I wonder if you'd give the children a treat. They'd love a visit from you and Prince."

Max hesitated, then his face broke into a wide grin. "Sure. I'd love to. Lead the way!"

"Carole and I can have a nice long chat," Mrs. Jones said, smiling at Mrs. Parker.

Max and Neil followed Nurse Williams out of the ward and down a short corridor.

"In here. This is the children's ward."

Neil looked around. The ward was brightly painted with pictures and posters on the walls. There were toys everywhere and a play area with a TV was down at the end of the ward. A little girl in the bed next to the door let out a shriek.

"It's Prince and Zeno! It's the time travelers!"

"It certainly is, Linda," Nurse Williams said, smiling. "Let's go down to the play area and you can hear all about your favorite TV show."

The children who were able to leave their beds gathered around, and soon Max was answering questions about the program and giving autographs. Prince received a lot of attention, too, with everybody wanting to stroke and pet him.

"Oh, you're so lucky," said a little boy in a wheelchair. "I wish I had a dog like Prince."

"We could adopt Prince," Linda said suddenly. "He could be our mascot."

"You could send us pictures of him from all the different places you visit," said another child excitedly.

Nurse Williams smiled. "I don't know how Max would feel about that."

Max's face fell. "Sorry, but Prince won't be in the show any longer."

Neil could see that Max was upset.

"Why is that?" Nurse Williams looked confused.

Max explained.

"But he's such a well-behaved dog," Nurse Williams said, after hearing the story.

"They *can't* take him out of the show," said the little boy in the wheelchair. "It wouldn't be the same."

"I'm going to call up the TV station and tell them not to fire Prince," Linda said, angrily.

Nurse Williams laughed. "Calm down, Linda. You probably would do it, too!"

A quiet, dark-haired boy looked up. "We could all sign a petition. We'll tell them Prince is our mascot and we want him to stay in the show."

The other children cheered and nodded in agreement. "I'll go and get a pencil," Linda said. "We can start right now."

Nurse Williams shook her head. "You've really given them something to think about now, Max." She looked at her watch. "It's nearly snack time. Maybe we should go back to Mrs. Jones."

Max and Neil waved good-bye to the children. They were all in a huddle around Linda, trying to decide what to say in their petition.

"And Prince really is our mascot?" the little boy in the wheelchair called out.

Max nodded. "I'll send you a picture of him."

"And one of you," Linda added.

"OK." Max smiled. "And I'll bring Prince back again if I can."

"What about *that*?" said Neil as he and Max made their way back to Mrs. Jones's ward. "You've got a fan club, Max."

Max shrugged. "Prince has."

"Do you really think they'll send a petition?"

Max shook his head. "Even if they did, what good would it do? You heard Jeff. He doesn't want to listen to kids."

"That's pretty ridiculous for somebody who makes kids' TV programs," Neil said angrily. "Anyway, we haven't talked to Dad about it yet. We'll do that tonight."

"Has Prince ever shown signs of disobedience *before* coming to Padsham Castle?" Mr. Parker asked later that evening.

Max shook his head. "He was great with his other trainer. It was just when Mr. Jenkins came that he started acting up."

"So he *has* been acting up?" Mr. Parker said thoughtfully.

"A bit, I suppose," Max admitted. "But Mr. Jenkins doesn't handle him properly. It sounds crazy, but he seems nervous around Prince."

"It certainly *does* sound crazy," Mr. Parker agreed. He thought for a moment. "I tell you what. Let's get Kate to try Prince out tomorrow. Prince hasn't met Kate yet. She had a day off today and she was gone

when you came home last night. She's a good dog-
handler, and if Prince behaves for her the first time
he meets her, then it isn't Prince we have to worry
about."

"It's a deal," Max said, looking relieved. "But I just
know it isn't Prince's fault."

"Down, boy," Kate said firmly. "Lie down."

Prince lay perfectly still while Kate walked across
the courtyard. Sam came bounding out of the house
to see what was going on. Neil made a move toward
him, but his father put a hand on his arm.

"Leave him alone," Bob Parker said quietly. "Let's
see how Prince handles this."

The Border collie trotted over to Prince and
barked. Neil watched Prince. The cocker spaniel's
eyes were fixed on Kate. He didn't move a muscle,
even when Sam nudged him on the flank.

"Sit!" Kate ordered.

Prince shifted to the sitting position in one fluid
movement. His eyes were still on Kate.

Sam flopped his head over on one side and wagged
his tail. The tip of Sam's tail caught the other dog on
the nose, but Prince still kept his eyes on Kate.

"Here, boy!" Kate called.

Prince leaped up excitedly.

"Walk!" said Kate.

Prince, instantly controlled, walked toward her.

She leaned down and gave him a pat. "Good boy! Very good, Prince."

Prince wagged his tail as Kate stood up again. Sam barked. Prince looked up at Kate and she smiled.

"OK, Prince. Go ahead!"

The two dogs raced off together across the court-yard.

Kate shrugged. "Perfect," she said as she came over to Mr. Parker.

Bob Parker nodded. "That's what I thought. So now we know where the problem lies."

"With Jenkins," Max said angrily. "I knew it all along."

"It seems you were right," said Bob Parker. "But what exactly *is* his problem?"

Max shrugged. "I don't care what his problem is. All I know is that if we don't persuade Jeff that it isn't Prince's fault, then he's going to get rid of him."

"You could talk to him, couldn't you, Dad?" Neil asked anxiously. "Convince him Jenkins is hiding something."

"I could." Bob Parker was thinking hard. "But I don't like to interfere, and if Prince has to work with Mr. Jenkins, then we still have a problem."

"Time's running out, though," Max chipped in. "I know Jeff wants to start shooting at the castle again tomorrow. We've got to do something. We can't give up."

"Why don't we ask Jeff to give Prince one last chance?" suggested Neil.

Max shook his head. "It's no good. Prince won't work for Mr. Jenkins."

"I wasn't thinking of him working with Mr. Jenkins," Neil said slowly. "I was thinking of asking Jeff to try him out with a different trainer."

"Who?" said Max. "We haven't got another trainer."

Neil turned to Kate and smiled. "Yes, we have. A brilliant one. Kate!"

Max's face lit up and he looked pleadingly at the King Street kennel assistant. "Kate?"

"But I've never done anything like that before." Kate was taken aback by the suggestion.

"You were great with Prince," Neil reasoned. "It might be our only chance."

Kate looked doubtful. "What do *you* think, Bob?"

"Jenkins isn't going to be too happy about it, that's for sure. But it might work," Mr. Parker said.

Kate looked at Prince romping with Sam on the other side of the courtyard. Then she looked at Max.

"OK, I'll try."

Max threw his arms around Kate. "Thanks! Thanks a million."

"Don't thank me yet," Kate said, laughing. She shook her head until her ponytail bobbed. "What have I gotten myself into?"

Neil grinned. "You can do it, Kate. I know you can do it."

CHAPTER EIGHT

Jeff Calton came around to King Street Kennels early on Wednesday morning to check that Max was fit and ready for the day's shooting ahead. He parked his car in the driveway and walked around to the back of the house. Everyone was in the kitchen eating toast.

The producer poked his head through the open door. "How's my star performer? Is he ready? You should be leaving soon."

Max crammed another piece of bread into his mouth and mumbled, "Nearly!"

"Have you found another Prince yet?"

Everyone looked at Sarah. She'd blurted out what was on everyone's mind before anybody else had the chance.

Jeff Calton sighed. "Yes. The agency has come up with a couple of dogs they think might do."

"They'll never be as good as Prince," said Max defensively.

The TV producer ran a hand through his hair. He looked stressed again. "Look, Max, I know how much Prince means to you, but I've got a deadline to meet. We've a long way to go in getting this episode filmed and we're already behind schedule. I just can't afford any more delays because Prince won't cooperate. Try to understand."

Max's mouth set in a stubborn line and Neil pushed his chair back and stood up.

"Can you give Prince just one more chance? He's fine now."

"He's had all the chances I can afford," Jeff said, shaking his head. "It's going to be a hectic day. We're going to pick up with the scene where Sir Gareth rides up to the castle."

Neil bit his lip. "It's still early though, isn't it?" he said.

Jeff nodded, looking puzzled.

"So we'll have time to bring Prince to the castle and let you see him rehearse a scene?" said Neil.

Max looked eagerly at Jeff. "That wouldn't hold you back much."

"I suppose not." Jeff sounded undecided. Then he sighed and shook his head. "It's a waste of time. Let it go, Max."

Max looked close to tears. Neil was disappointed, too.

Jeff looked at Max, concerned. Then his face changed as he looked around and caught sight of Kate walking Fred across the courtyard toward them.

"Wow! What a magnificent dog!"

"That's Fred," said Neil proudly. "That's the Irish wolfhound I was telling you about."

Jeff suddenly seemed very interested. "Is that his owner?"

Max shook his head. "That's Kate, the kennel assistant."

"She certainly knows how to handle a dog. Look how Fred is following her. He doesn't look the least bit dangerous."

Neil looked. Fred was loping along beside Kate, his feet lifting high and head held steady, looking straight ahead.

Neil jumped in. "Kate is very good with dogs. She was going to bring Prince to the castle."

"So you had this all planned?"

Neil blushed but Jeff was thinking hard.

"You know that idea you had, Neil?"

"You mean about Sir Gareth having a war hound? I thought it would look great if Sir Gareth rode up to the castle with Fred trotting along beside him."

Then Jeff scratched his head. "I don't suppose you know where I would find his owner, do you?"

Neil's mouth dropped open. "You mean you want to use him, after all? Mr. Grey would be thrilled. I know he would."

"Grey," said Jeff, writing the name down on a scrap of paper. "And where can I find him?"

"I think he's coming to pick up Fred this afternoon. Kate could tell you."

Jeff looked at them. "Wait here. And *don't* go away."

Max and Neil looked at each other.

"This could be really fantastic!" Neil said excitedly.

"And it could mean Jeff will give Prince one last chance. If he's in a good mood, there's still hope."

Neil watched as Jeff had a word with Kate. Then he saw the producer take his cell phone out of his pocket and make a call. He spoke for a few moments, then handed the phone to Kate. She spoke into it. She was nodding her head and obviously answering questions.

Jeff was grinning as he walked back toward the boys.

"Look, here's the deal. I've just spoken to Mr. Grey and he's agreed we can use Fred, so long as Kate comes with him. He'll meet us at the castle later." He paused and looked directly at Max. "Kate says she might as well bring both dogs along."

It took a moment for it to sink in.

"You mean Prince?" Max said.

Jeff nodded. "But don't go getting your hopes up, Max. If either one of these other dogs from the agency is any good, I'll take it."

"You won't want to," said Max confidently. "Not after you've seen Prince again."

Jeff shook his head, laughing. "Talk about stubborn."

Neil's mouth was hanging open. "What made you change your mind?"

Jeff smiled. "I reckoned I owed you a favor. If your idea about using Fred works out, it's really going to add something special to one of the key scenes." His eyes took on a dreamy look. "I can see it now. I think we'll have the horses coming out of some mist. Then you'll see Fred. It'll be great. Brian will love it."

Jeff was still talking about the shot as he got into his car and drove away. Kate came toward them with Fred at her side.

Max turned to Neil. "It was you who changed his mind. Thanks for having that brilliant idea about Fred."

Neil grinned. "So now it's all systems go. C'mon, we've got to get ready. Keep your fingers crossed it'll all turn out OK." He rubbed Fred's ears. The big dog turned his head toward Neil's hand and his mouth lolled open. Fred loved the attention. "You're going to be a star, Fred — just like Prince. Isn't it great?"

Fred gave a friendly bark on cue and everyone laughed.

Kate tutted. "And now I'm taking two dogs instead of one. I must be crazy."

"Crazy about dogs," said Neil. "Like us!"

Kate drove Max, Neil, and Emily over to Padsham Castle with the two dogs.

"I'm really getting used to this." Neil jumped down from the Range Rover.

Emily looked around, then pointed toward the drawbridge. "There's Jeff. And Brian."

They were both talking to a couple of cameramen

as Brian lined up a shot of the drawbridge. Another man was close by, clutching a machine with a long tube.

"Put the mist machine over there," Brian said to him as Max and Neil ran up. "Make sure it's well out of shot. Where's the sound engineer? I need to talk to him."

Jeff turned just as Kate and Emily arrived with the dogs.

"Hi, you guys. Wow!" Brian gave Fred a friendly pat. "I'm really looking forward to seeing how this shot goes. We're getting the mist machine set up. You were right, Jeff. This *is* going to be something special. We'll be ready for the run-through in fifteen."

Fred raised his elegant muzzle and looked around him. The wolfhound wasn't in the least disturbed by all the activity. "What a dog!" Brian said before turning back to the cameramen.

Max hopped impatiently from foot to foot. "What about Prince?"

Jeff smiled. "Bring him over here out of Brian's way. We can try him out with a couple of moves. But remember, I'm making no promises."

"What about trying the scene where I get my cape caught on the drawbridge and Prince unhooks it?" said Max.

"OK," said Jeff. "Go and get into costume."

"I'd better go, too," said Emily. "Are you coming, Neil?"

Neil shook his head. "I can slip mine on over my jeans and T-shirt. Can you get it for me?"

Emily nodded and she and Max ran off to the wardrobe trailer. As they went, Neil saw a man approaching with two cocker spaniels.

"They look just like Prince!"

"That's the idea," said Jeff, raising his eyebrows. "I have to find a dog that looks exactly the same."

The man walked up to them. "Hi. I'm Phil Bolton. Where do you want me to show you the dogs?"

The producer looked around. "Here, if you like. There's a space just in front of the light rig." Then he turned to Kate and Neil. "Hang on a few more minutes, will you? I should see to these two first. Prince will have to wait a little longer."

Neil and Kate exchanged anxious glances. Neil looked over at some of the light stands on the lawn. They stood about two feet high and had big flaps around the lights so that the beams could be directed where the cameras needed it. Cables trailed from them, snaking over the grass to one of the TV company's big generator vans.

"Can I watch?" asked Kate. "I'd like to see a real trainer at work. I might get some tips."

"I'm not really a trainer," the man said. "I thought *you* were the trainer."

Kate looked at Prince and Fred by her side. "Oh, no. I'm a kennel assistant."

"Our own trainer will be along any minute," said

Jeff, looking at his watch. "He's a bit late this morning. At the moment all I want to see is if your dogs can obey basic commands."

Neil watched as the dogs were put through their paces and his heart quickly sank into his boots. The dogs behaved well — especially compared to Prince, who kept tugging at his leash, dragging on it, and whining.

"Quiet, Prince," Kate said firmly.

Jeff glanced across. "He still isn't behaving himself, is he?"

Kate shook her head. "I don't know what's got into him. He hasn't done this with me before."

Max rushed up, cape flying from his shoulders.

"That was quick," said Neil.

Max grinned. "I don't have to line up!"

"Like the extras! Are Chris and Hasheem here yet?"

Max nodded. "Julie, too. They're with Emily. Is Jeff ready to do the scene?" Then his face froze as he looked at the other two dogs. They looked like replicas of Prince and they were both behaving beautifully — coming to heel and sitting when told.

Prince barked and dragged his leash so hard Kate lost hold of it. At once Prince was off, around the back of the light stands, in among the wires and cables, barking furiously.

Jeff looked at him and shook his head. "There isn't

any point trying him out. Look at him. He's out of control."

Neil and Max glared at Prince. He was standing, feet planted firmly on either side of a trailing wire, barking and howling.

Max was at a loss for words. "I don't understand. I just don't understand."

"I do." Jeff's face was set like stone. "You can't say it's Mr. Jenkins's fault now, can you, Max? He's not even here. Prince is finished. My only problem now is to decide which of these two dogs to choose."

CHAPTER NINE

Neil was devastated. "Come on, Max. We might as well give up."

Max nodded and together the boys walked toward Prince. The cocker spaniel's barking grew even more frenzied, but when Max put a hand on his collar, he wouldn't move.

Even Max began losing patience with the dog. "Come on, Prince!"

Neil was looking intently at Prince. "Wait a minute. *Why* won't he move?"

"Because Jeff is right, Neil. He won't do as he's told."

"That isn't true, though. We know that. He was fine this morning. And look at Fred, he's not moving a muscle!"

The big shaggy dog was calm, unmoved by the noise Prince was making.

Neil got down beside Prince and put a hand on his neck. "What is it, boy? What's wrong?"

Kate and Max looked on, anxiously.

Neil's other hand brushed a cable at his feet and he drew it back sharply. "Ouch!"

"What?" said Max.

"The cable's hot," gasped Neil. As he looked at the cable, a thin wisp of smoke rose from it. "It's smoldering," Neil said. "It's on fire."

Then Jeff heard him. "What was that? Get out of there, Neil. Right away!"

"Prince won't budge," said Neil.

But Jeff was already yelling to a runner. "Get a sparky, someone. We need a technician right away! And pull the plug on this light stand. Hurry, man!"

The runner tore off toward one of the trailers. Seconds later another man in blue overalls came hurtling out of the trailer and was down on his knees beside the cable.

Max and Neil dragged Prince away and tried to settle him down next to where Fred was sitting. Prince kept barking at the man beside the cable.

Jeff's face was white. "What's up?"

The technician looked up. "It looks like a short circuit. Keep everybody away while I get it sorted out."

"Is it fixable?"

"Just about. I'll have to rewire the whole stand. It

looks as if the wires are slow burning inside the casing. It was only a matter of time before the casing burned through. Anybody who touched it would have been in real trouble."

"Electrocuted?" Jeff looked appalled.

Already a crowd had started to gather. Chris and Hasheem heard the commotion and came running up. Julie and Emily were close on their heels. They were already in costume.

"What's going on?" asked Emily, concerned.

Neil filled her in. "There's something wrong with the lights. They could have blown up."

"Keep back," Jeff warned. He turned to Max. "Thank goodness Prince started acting up."

"Wait a minute," said the man with the two cocker spaniels. "I think it was a bit more than that."

"What do you mean?" Jeff sounded surprised.

"It looks to me as if Prince smelled the cable burning."

Max jumped in. "He was warning us. I told you Prince was clever."

Jeff's mouth gaped open. "Well, if that's true, I certainly owe him an apology."

"If the light had blown, it would have been a disaster!" Neil gasped.

"Somebody might have been *hurt* . . ." said Jeff, looking worried.

"You see, he *wasn't* misbehaving," pleaded Max. "Give him another try, please, Jeff."

The big wolfhound barked twice as if in agreement.

Chris coughed to get everybody's attention, then he looked at Jeff. "I've got something for you. My mom was at the hospital today. Mrs. Jones is coming home tomorrow."

"That's great." Jeff smiled.

"The nurse on the children's ward gave Mom this. It's for you."

Chris held out a pink envelope with a picture of some elephants on it.

Jeff looked at the envelope in disbelief. "Elephants? Er, are you sure this is for me?"

Chris nodded. "Positive."

Jeff opened the envelope and took out several sheets of paper. They seemed to be covered in names. The producer ran a hand through his hair and laughed. "Well, I never."

"What?" said Max.

"You know what this is?" Jeff asked.

Max shook his head.

"It's a petition from the children's ward at the hospital. You've got them all on your side, Max."

"Everybody likes Prince. He's OK. I've been trying to tell you that. Nobody wants to see him go."

"So I can see! Well, maybe we *will* have to give Prince that trial after all."

"*Yes!*" said Max, punching the air. "I'll go and set things up on the drawbridge. You tell Kate what she has to do. And don't be long!"

Neil watched as Max ran toward the castle.

"Here," said Kate, handing Fred's leash to Neil. "Wish me luck."

"Jenkins hasn't shown up yet, so I'll take you through things myself. Now what Prince has to do is . . ." Jeff began, walking across the lawn with Kate and Prince. The dog walked calmly at Kate's heels.

"What was all that about?" asked Hasheem, scratching his head. He bent down and ruffled Fred's ears.

Neil explained while they watched Prince go through the scene. It was perfect. The cocker spaniel ran across the drawbridge in front of Max, then Max fell and his cape got caught. Then Prince had to run back and free him.

"Look at that," said the man with the spaniels. "It would take my dogs ages to learn to do that."

Max came racing across the grass to them with Prince in hot pursuit. "Perfect!" he cried.

Neil nodded. "Great stuff, Max. And well done, Prince!"

"But can we be sure he'll be reliable?" said Jeff a moment later as he reached them.

"He was reliable with me," Kate confirmed.

Jeff still looked worried. He looked up. "Here's Harry Jenkins. Let's see what he thinks."

Jenkins was coming in through the castle gates. He walked slowly across the lawn toward them. His eyes were fixed on Fred. Neil stared at him and followed his eyes. The man seemed transfixed by the sight of the wolfhound.

There was a shout from the castle gates. A short, stocky man was hurrying through them behind Jenkins. Fred started forward and barked once. Then the dog looked up at Neil.

"It's Mr. Grey," said Kate. "Fred's owner."

Neil bent down to Fred and unclipped his leash. "Go on, boy," he whispered. "Go to your master."

The huge wolfhound leaped forward and began to run in great loping strides toward his master — and toward Harry Jenkins.

The dog trainer immediately put his arms up in

front of his face. "Get it away from me," he yelled. "Call that dog off!"

Fred hesitated a moment, then continued toward his owner, straight past Jenkins.

Neil looked at the terrified man staggering toward them. The trainer turned and dropped his arms. His face was chalk-white.

"What on earth is the matter?" Jeff said, running up to him. "Are you sick or something? The dog was nowhere near you. It was running past you, man."

Jenkins gritted his teeth. "I thought it was going for me."

Jeff's eyes narrowed. "You were scared by a dog? But you're a dog *trainer*!"

Jenkins nodded and didn't look at anybody. Neil noticed that he was rubbing his arm again. Neil had seen him do that before.

Jeff probed further. "You stepped in to cover on *The Time Travelers* because I thought you were one of the best dog trainers around. I trusted your judgment!"

"I *used* to be one of the best," Harry Jenkins said guiltily. He had the look on his face of a man who had just been found out.

"What do you mean?"

"I was very badly bitten on the arm by an Alsatian a couple of months ago. It got to me. This is my first job since. I thought I would be OK with a cocker spaniel."

"But you clearly aren't, are you?" Jeff was obviously furious.

Jenkins shook his head. "I was coming to tell you anyway. I've been sick this morning just thinking about it. I don't think I can do the show any longer."

Neil and Max exchanged unbelieving looks.

Max wanted answers, too. "You kept blaming Prince, Mr. Jenkins."

The man looked thoroughly miserable. "I know. I'm sorry. A dog senses when a trainer is nervous. I should have known. It isn't Prince's fault. It's mine. I've handled everything so badly."

Jeff was furious. "I don't believe it! This is just what I need right now."

Neil swallowed. He was beginning to feel sorry for the trainer. "Look, Mr. Jenkins. Just because one dog bit you, that doesn't mean it's going to happen again. I mean, I'm sure you could do *something* about getting your confidence back."

Jenkins nodded. "I know. I'm thinking things through now. But I need time off regardless. You'll need to find another trainer, Jeff."

"You should have told me," Jeff said stonily. "I can't be expected to do everybody's job as well as mine."

"I'm sorry." Jenkins turned away and began to walk back toward the castle gate. As he passed Max and Prince he gave a weak smile and patted the golden cocker spaniel affectionately on the head. Then he left.

Max laid a hand on the producer's arm. He'd softened a little bit. "I feel sorry for Mr. Jenkins. I mean, it was really brave of him to carry on working with Prince when he was feeling so uncomfortable, wasn't it?"

"I suppose so." Jeff shook his head. "And it was you who kept saying it wasn't Prince's fault. You're the one who should be feeling annoyed."

"I'm not angry. I'm just glad Prince has got his job back."

"Prince is saved!" Chris patted Max on the back and Hasheem joined in. As Neil and Kate congratulated Max, too, shaking him energetically by the hand, Prince's tail thumped on the grass. He knew everyone was happy and he was determined to join in.

"Speaking of jobs," said Jeff, interrupting the celebrations, "I could use another trainer." He turned to Kate. "I don't suppose you want a job with a TV production company, do you, Kate?"

Neil held his breath. Kate would never leave King Street Kennels, would she?

Kate laughed. "I've *got* a job," she said. "A job that I love." She winked at Neil. "I wouldn't leave King Street for anything. But I'll help you out this afternoon. How's that?"

"Great," said Jeff, grinning. "Now, let's introduce

Fred to Sir Gareth. This is going to be a great shot! Brian is really excited about it."

Kate went to meet Mr. Grey. Fred was obviously overjoyed to see his master again, and poor Mr. Grey was having a hard time keeping his balance while Fred put his front paws on the little man's shoulders. Neil hoped Kate could get Fred calm enough for the shot. Somehow, he knew she would.

Neil turned to watch as Jeff set off with a determined walk toward the drawbridge. Brian Mason was standing by, conducting the cast and crew, waving his hands in the air, and talking to three people at once — about different things!

The man with the cocker spaniels looked at Neil. "I guess I'm done. I'd better get back."

Neil bit his lip. "It isn't that there's anything wrong with your dogs, Mr. Bolton," he said, bending down to stroke the spaniels' floppy ears.

"I know that," said the man. "They've been in tons of ads and TV dramas before. But to tell the truth, these two are twins and they hate being apart. So maybe it's for the best."

"Maybe it is," said Neil as the two dogs licked his face.

He could hear Brian shouting in the distance. "Get that mist machine going! Where's Sir Gareth? Max, get on that pony! Extras! Where is my crowd? Come *on*! We haven't got all day. Good boy, Prince! Thank

goodness somebody knows what they're doing around here!"

Neil ran toward the wardrobe trailer and scrambled into his costume. Kate was already at the drawbridge, leading Fred to stand beside Sir Gareth's horse. Mr. Grey was standing some way off, watching proudly.

Chris waved at Neil. "Come on!"

Brian was still shouting. His voice rebounded off the castle walls as Neil skidded into place beside Emily and the others.

"Ready, Sir Gareth? Kate, Fred looks wonderful! Start the mist — and — *action!*"

CHAPTER TEN

Sir Gareth rode out of the mist, his faithful war hound loping along beside him. Behind him, on a small gray pony, rode Zeno, with Prince at his side. The castle loomed out of the swirling mist, and at a window in the topmost tower, a face appeared. It was the Lady Genevieve, imprisoned by the wicked Baron Dredmore.

The riders reined in their mounts and Prince let out a sharp bark. At once the ground was alive with figures, appearing from nowhere out of the mist, gathering silently around the riders.

Sir Gareth raised his lance and pointed to the drawbridge. The villagers closed in behind the riders as Sir Gareth and Zeno rode their horses across the *bridge. A cry of warning went up from the castle but it was too late. The villagers raised their voices in a great roar of triumph and charged!*

"Wow!" Neil whispered. "It *does* look great."

"There *we* are!" Chris was pointing at the large screen in his excitement.

"Oh, look!" Emily cried. "Isn't it weird seeing yourself on TV?"

The little preview suite at Prince Productions in Manchester was crammed with people. In addition to Max and all the rest of the actors, there were some of the extras from Meadowbank School, Max's parents, Bob and Carole Parker and Sarah, Mr. Grey, and, of course, Mrs. Jones. The dogs were there, too — including Toby, who got pretty excited when he saw Prince on the screen.

"Down with Baron Dredmore!" yelled the extras on screen, and Neil was tempted to join in.

There were also a few special guests of honor. Jeff had invited some of the children who'd been in Compton Hospital. Nurse Williams came, too — and she was just as excited.

The time tunnel appeared on screen and Zeno and Prince disappeared into it. The theme music played and the titles rolled. The lights came up and everybody sat back.

"That was great!" said Julie excitedly.

"It was fantastic!" agreed Hasheem. "I'm definitely going to be an actor when I grow up."

"You already *are* an actor," mocked Chris. "At least, according to Mr. Hamley."

Jeff stood up in the front row and faced the audience. "Well, I hope you all enjoyed that!"

The room suddenly erupted with a loud chorus of shouts and cheers.

"Don't forget that there's food laid out next door, everybody," Jeff said when everyone was finally quiet again.

Chris grinned. "Great! I'm starving."

"First though, I've got a few people to thank," Jeff went on. "Most importantly, King Street Kennels. If it hadn't been for King Street, and especially Neil, Prince might have been out of a job and we'd have lost a really great doggy star."

"Hear! Hear!" Max yelled. "Let's hear it for King Street and the Puppy Patrol!"

There was more loud cheering and Jeff had to raise his voice to make himself heard. "Then there's Kate and Fred."

Neil turned around and smiled at Kate and Mr. Grey. Fred was sitting between them.

"Imagine my Fred being a star," said Mr. Grey proudly. "I'm going to get a photograph from Prince Productions to put up in the shop."

"A framed photograph," said Jeff, laughing. "And if I ever need an Irish wolfhound again . . ."

"You just come to me and Fred," said Mr. Grey, laying a hand on the wolfhound's shaggy head.

Fred looked up at him and Neil smiled.

"I'm also keeping Toby in mind," Jeff said, pointing to the old lady and her little dog in the fifth row.

Mrs. Jones laughed. "I don't think my Toby's got star quality. But he suits me fine!"

Jeff had sent a car for Mrs. Jones. She still had to use crutches, but her leg was on the mend.

"There's one more announcement," said Jeff above the laughter. "But I think I'll let Brian make that one, since the person who thought it up is too shy to do it."

Brian leaped to his feet and stood beside Jeff. He was holding a piece of pink paper in his hand. "This is the petition from the children at the hospital."

Emily cheered and the children joined in.

"Jeff and I are going to keep this," Brian went on. "In fact we're going to put it on our office wall — just to remind us that we should always listen to what *The Time Travelers'* fans say."

"I'm for that," Julie shouted out, then blushed.

"And we're going to have the biggest fund-raiser ever for the children's ward at Compton. There's going to be a summer fun day out at Padsham Castle to benefit the hospital — with the stars of all your favorite TV shows. You'll be very impressed when you see the lineup we've got for you."

"Awesome!" Neil laughed and turned to Max. "That was a great idea."

Max's jaw dropped. "How did you know it was *my* idea?"

Neil gave him a shove. "Don't be foolish," he said. "It's exactly the kind of thing you'd think of. You're a star!"

Max shook his head and looked around. "Not me! It was you and the hospital and Kate and all the rest who really cared who saved Prince. You're the stars."

"And so is Prince," added Neil.

"Oh, definitely. Prince is a star, all right, aren't you, boy?"

Prince looked up and thumped his tail on the floor.

A tall man with dark hair stood up. "I've also got something to say," he said.

"Dad?" said Max, puzzled.

Max's dad smiled at him, then turned to face the other, expectant faces. "I've got a surprise for Max. His mom and I didn't realize just how fond he was of Prince."

Neil looked at the woman sitting next to Max. She smiled at her son as he looked inquiringly at her.

"What's going on?" mouthed Max.

"Wait and see," his mom whispered.

"To make a long story short," Max's dad continued, "we've been in touch with the animal agency — and they're going to *sell* Prince. To Max."

Max's mouth hung open. He looked too shocked to speak.

"Well, say something," said his mom, with a wide grin.

Max looked at his parents, then at Prince.

"Mine?" Max couldn't believe it. "Prince is really mine?"

Prince looked up at him and barked. Max put his arms round the cocker spaniel's neck.

"Did you hear that, Prince?" he said. "Now we'll always be together."

Neil looked at Max's parents. "I think he's pleased."

Everybody laughed.

"Food, anybody?" said Brian.

There was a cheer and a mad rush for the door — dogs as well as children.

After all, Neil thought, looking at Max and Prince — even stars have to eat!